Sol Azure

Xurek Akun

Sol Azure

ISBN: 978-0615868431

Printed 2014

For information: khalidbey93@gmail.com

Cover illustration by Khalid El Bey

Published by

DEYEL PUBLISHING

217 West Kennedy Street, Syracuse, New York [13205]

CREATIVE RESEARCH SOCIETY

Syracuse New York

Printed in the United States of America.

Other Books Published by Deyel Publishing

The Key to Character

The African American Dilemma

Now

From My Eyes; Community Memoirs

Necessary Adjustments

To the members of my Organization....keep searching.

Sol Azure

Number one – **My reluctance**

Often times I sit back and I reflect on the many strange happenings that I have experienced over the course of my life. You, just like me, have often been alone and thought you might have seen movement in your peripheral. Or, you may have experienced déjà vu; where you sensed that you have lived a certain circumstance before. Or, you may have even been asleep and felt as if you were falling. Or you felt such an eerie feeling, that the hairs stood up on the back of your neck; as if someone or 'something' had just entered the room where you were. We have all experienced these types, as well as other types of strange happenings, maybe even more than once.

Nothing that I have ever experienced though, is as strange as the story that I am about to share with you in a moment.

Initially, I wasn't sure if I should share this story with anyone. The ideas that I have considered sharing are so strange and difficult to describe, that I feared the reader would write me off as crazy, or as a sensationalist desirous of attention and reputation. These things that I am about to describe took place over a seven year time span, beginning about 14 or so years ago. Strangely enough, though the events that I am about to mention have taken place about 14 or so years ago, it is my opinion and/or belief that said events have had an effect on me even beyond those seven years; maybe even today.

I hope that you find my story interesting; maybe enlightening. Who knows, there may be some of you who can relate to my experiences. Some of you may have even lived similar or the same experiences.

As mentioned, I was once very hesitant to share my story; but I am not hesitant anymore…... and so, it begins.

Number two – **A beginning**

I am not going to bore you with the typical story beginning about my life as a child or about who or how my parents were. I am not going to identify my location nor make known my nativity; and my name is irrelevant. I am currently 34 years of age. I am of a certain coffee colored persuasion, and I reside somewhere on the planet Earth. How's that for an opening? What "is" important or relevant is what I am about to communicate you.

In the not too distant past I had developed an interest in most things mysterious; I say most, instead of all, because there are some things that are just not worth knowing. I would read about religion and history; I would read about religions' effect on history. I would read about old and ancient cultures and their religious or spiritual beliefs and practices. I would wonder about the connection between the more current religions and the religions of old. I wondered about whether the teachings of the various religions were true and whether the governments of the world knew the truth behind religion; if such a truth did in fact exist.

My quest to understand religion led me to other things, practices or ideas that religion often condemned. It was a bit peculiar, because most of the ideas condemned by religion seemed quite religious themselves.

One day I came across a piece of information that would forever change my thoughts and/or ideas about religion. This piece of information suggested that the religious texts of the world were no more than metaphorical personifications of certain happenings in nature. The information suggested that the many religious texts of the world were mere plagiarized versions of the Egyptian stories of Osiris, Isis, and Horus. I thought "wow". An understanding that the assumed Egyptian mystery was about the sun disk or about the power hidden behind the sun disk caused me to determine that maybe the religious texts of the world too were about the sun as well. As a result of this assumption I begin to read certain popular religious texts. I also simultaneously begin to study astronomy and astrology. My study of astrology led me to study other similar subject matters; including numerology, tarot, and uncommon subjects of study that endeavored to understand the influence that the unseen might have on the seen. In other words, these subject matters that are considered or labeled occult subject matters are the investigation of the effect that unseen forces have on the physical world. I always found it interesting that the religions of the world suggested that these occult types of practices were somehow an evil hoax; but religion also seeks to determine the influence of unseen forces (i.e. "God") on physical world; quite the contradiction, wouldn't you say?

You often hear the sayings, "be careful what you wish for", or "seek and ye shall find".

Nothing could be truer. My study of astrology, along with my study of certain popular religious texts led me to realize that what was suggested by the information that I found was in fact true. These religious texts appeared to contain a host of hidden mysteries, veiled by or hidden behind a bunch of strange allegories; allegories are ideas or phrases that appear to communicate one message, but which in fact communicate one or more hidden messages. This discovery completely blew my mind. At this point I wanted to know more. I wanted to find out about everything that was hidden, not only in religious texts, but also behind or by government, secret societies, etc. From this point on I wanted to uncover any and every piece of secret knowledge there was.

My focus, my direction, my devotion, my life would be forever changed.

Number three – **The discovery**

It was shocking, disappointing, and exciting to learn that the religious texts of the world were communicating secret messages; secret messages that the everyday man and woman was or is totally unaware of. It was just as shocking to learn that those who have been or who claim to have been ordained clergyman of their respective religions were or are also unaware of the hidden messages in these religious texts. My continual search, not just within religious text, but into other references as well had led me to realize that the mystery lies behind or is hidden within the language.

What's known as the English language for example, or more correctly the English dialect was/is formulated from more ancient languages. In order to understand anything expressed in English, a person must look to a certain word's origin to determine its true or original meaning. For example, the word 'holy' is derived from the Greek word "*Helios*", which translates to "*Sun*". The word 'bible' is derived from the Greek word "*biblio*", which means "*book*". So in essence the cover of the holy Bible really reads "*Sun Book*"! This discovery blew my mind. From this point on, the more I read this 'Sun Book', the more I realized the many references to astrological principles within it. Let's take Ezekiel's Wheel as an example. This great wonder that appeared in the sky possessing the faces of a calf, a lion, an eagle, and a man, I thought, was a pretty strange story. It goes on to say that "*each beast had two wings; and each one's wing touches the others wing; and they turn not.*" Ironically, in the zodiac wheel there exists what is called the four fixed signs, which are Taurus, Leo, Scorpio, and Aquarius. I was looking at this and I begin to think, is it me or are these not the same exact symbols described in Ezekiel's wheel? Taurus or the face of a calf; Leo or the face of a lion; Scorpio or the face of the Eagle; and Aquarius or the face of a man. Even more revealing is the fact that each of these signs are considered "fixed", meaning they exist during the times when each of the four seasons (Spring, Summer, Fall, and Winter) are stable, or as it says in the Bible, they turn not; they don't change. Each fixed sign in the zodiac is flanked by two other signs. For example, to one side of Taurus you have the sign of Aries; and to the other side of Taurus you have the sign Gemini. To one side of Leo you have the sign of Cancer; and to the other side of Leo you have the sign of Virgo. When I looked at the two fixed signs of Taurus and Leo, I realized that metaphorically they each have "two wings" or they each have one sign on either side of them. I remembered that the Bible passage said that each one's wing touches the others wing; and I thought...hmmm. Gemini, which is a wing of Taurus touches Cancer, which is a wing of Leo. Virgo, which is a wing of Leo touches Libra, which is a wing of Scorpio; and so it continues this way all the way around the wheel! This was just one very obvious example of astrological principle that I found in this particular religious texts.

Realizing that the Bible and similar books essentially possessed buried treasures, I needed to know more. Since my study of a few occult topics assisted me in uncovering at least one mystery in the religious texts, I figured that I needed to learn more occult sciences. As I mentioned earlier I begin to read about and practice the tarot. I then began to also study and practice numerology. I began to study eastern philosophies like I Ching and Taoism. I even began studying and practicing elemental spiritual practices. During the course of my study I realized that all of these so-called occult subjects were essentially discussing the same principles; their apparent differences being only their cultural sources. What was even more strange was the fact that certain principles of even these occult subjects, I found in the religious texts. In fact, the religious texts appeared to be almost a compilation of occult principles buried behind what appears to be old folktales!

After a period of time I begin to turn my attention away from the religious texts and focus more on occult and spiritual practices. I begin to meditate more and I often tried and succeeded at predicting future events in my life using numerology, tarot, but most of the time, astrology.

I remember back in my younger years hearing religious persons talk about how occult practices such as astrology were the works of the devil or devil worship. I remember hearing how science argued that astrology's claims could not be validated. I think about it in the present moment, having done predictions myself I wonder, why would they lie? Why would they deprive humanity of the ability foresee events? Or even better, why deprive us all of the ability to foresee and thereby avoid negative events? I remember thinking "what is the big deal"? I became very disappointed in religion and in government. I say government, because governments funds science. Having had some success with predictions via these occult sciences I just could not understand why these "tools", which could be used for making discoveries, and which appeared to have been left behind by our ancient ancestors 'for us' were so off-limits. Then... It happened.

Number four – **And then there was light**

My desire to know motivated me every single day to search for what could qualify as truth. I plunged myself deeper and deeper into occult practices. While astrology was my main practice, I began to experiment more and more with elemental spiritual practices. As one might imagine, initially the motivations were selfish. Earthly ideas or accomplishments were what occupied my mind; but as my understanding improved, what I came to want more than anything else in the world, was simply to 'know more' or to understand more (about life).

I remember reading a few books about ancient Egyptian concepts or ideals. I remember coming across a discussion about the Sphinx. So many explorers from all around the world worked very hard to crack the Riddle of the Sphinx. As it stands this Riddle has been cracked long ago by those who were qualified, but I am simply mentioning this for the sake of my story. The Riddle of the Sphinx goes as follows: "What is that which in the morning goeth upon four feet; upon two feet in the afternoon; and in the Evening upon three?" Most people who considered this riddle thought that this riddle referred to the ages of man; when in fact it made reference to the four elements, within two hemispheres, manifesting via a heavenly Trinity. I discovered though, interestingly enough that despite the idea of this riddle not representing the ages of man (necessarily), it essentially culminates in man. This discovery brought to mind the Egyptian proverb, "know thyself". This suggestion made by the ancient Egyptians to know thyself calls on the 'beginner' to learn and know his nativity; his origin. I remember asking myself "wow, is this suggesting that we know our family origins, our national origins, our genetic origins?" I thought that such a consideration was strange indeed, for what man does not know himself? My continual practice of astrology confirmed that I and most others the planet are clueless about who we really are. The religious text of the world appeared to contradict one another in one respect; on one hand there are religious texts that suggest that man originates from sin; as if his very existence is an abomination. Then there are others that suggest that man has a divine origin; and that he is a reflection of divinity. The realization that these trustworthy references contradict each other might cause one to become quite confused. I on the other hand continued to compare notes to determine which statement was true. What I learned was that while man's origin is divine, he lives his life in sin. Do not allow yourself to get caught up in the ideas of good and evil. They are just extremes of the same phenomenon.

Realizing that man's origin was divine was a great lesson. From that moment on I attempted to perfect my thinking; eliminating negative thoughts one at a time, in an effort perfectly reflect divinity. It was interesting because I slowly begin to realize over time that the more and more I ridded my mind of negative constructs, the more I began to understand or see things that I did not understand or see before.

The combination of occult study and emotional and intellectual cleansing if you will empowered me with the ability to predict on-coming events in small measure; and I became especially adept in predicting human behavior. It is as if the air around me was polluted with hundreds of foreign particles, that my rose colored glasses prevented me from seeing. But once those glasses were removed, I slowly begin to notice how polluted the air really was.

This was an amazing discovery. At times I felt as if my eyes were growing in size and that my mind was 'weightless'. I came to realize that the mind was both active and passive simultaneously; that in normal circumstances, a person is usually cognizant of their active, concrete consciousness; but we are seldom aware that our mind is equally passive and is constantly absorbing from the environment which surrounds us. The realization that the mind works like a vacuum caused me to go deeper into occult studies. This period marks another significant change in my thinking and therefore my life.

Number 5 – **My initiation**

At this point I had made a number of discoveries. I learned the truth about my national origin. I learned the truth about my geographic origin. I learned truth about my psychological makeup, my behavior; and had made improvements. I learned a lot about my environment. I learned a lot about human behavior in general and the chief motivator of over 85% of the population. Though I had learned all of these things and more, I felt as though there was still something missing; something that I probably couldn't figure out through my independent study alone. So I begin to research and/or search out study groups or organizations that I thought might have either more information than me or means by which said information could be received.

My search led me to one particular organization that at least on the surface appeared to be a fountain of information. I spent some time in this organization, first suffering through its initiations; and then following its rules and procedures. 90% of persons involved in this organization were considerably older than I was. This dynamic made it a bit difficult to ascertain information. It was as if these more senior persons either had a fear of younger persons learning what they knew and surpassing them; or maybe they didn't trust young minds being in possession of such sensitive information. Further probing led me to discover that, what appeared to be very regal, intelligent, sources of information, was in fact just a bunch of people "playing the part" of what they wish they really were. By comparing my previous learnings with the information that I did receive in this organization, I realize that at least the immediate managers of this organization had absolutely no clue about what they were involved in. This finding was little disappointing. Here I spent all of this time and energy following their rules playing along, only to learn that the organization and its practices were hollow. Because of this I promptly drafted and submitted my letter of resignation and headed out in search of greener pastures.

Despite the fact that I learned that the organization with which I was affiliated was less thorough in its understanding than it was in its appearance, I did gather some very valuable information. And so though not necessarily back to square one, I was once again a man without a country. I was sitting in my home one day and I thought what better way to continue my search than to engage in the practices that led me here in the first place. So, I delve back into my occult practices.

I was reading my astrological chart and I made yet another discovery. What I discovered was that what an astrological chart displays to the reader is the never ending battle between fate and free will throughout the reader's life. Most people are familiar with the idea of fate and are convinced or condition the think that fate is all there is. The idea of fate suggests predictability. An event or circumstance becomes predictable only because it has occurred repeatedly, as with statistics. Persons who fail to control their emotional responses to circumstances become predictable. But it is when the person grabs hold of the emotional response in an effort to redirect his energy in a more productive direction that it can be said that free will has intervened or disrupted or "altered" fate. This idea excited me because it meant that man, his circumstance, and his life, can be as he wishes it or as he "wills" it to be. Once again my thinking and therefore my life was forever changed.

I wondered: how can I use my will to improve my life, or better yet, to receive what I have been in search of for several years now?

An idea!

I immediately ran to my room and begin to pull out and organize my tools that I used for my elemental spiritual practices. I perfectly worked out the details of what I wanted to say. I arranged my workstation in the appropriate manner. I thought for a moment. I then closed my eyes and I reached out into the void with the hopes of finding a spark of light.

What did I reach for you say?

What I reached for was a greater understanding of the environment that surrounds me; a greater understanding of life and the power that animates it. I wanted to know if there was anything lying behind the veil of space; and if there was anything lying behind the veil of space, I wanted to know what it was. What I reached for was a greater, more in depth occult knowledge and understanding. As I said earlier, be careful or at least be cautious about what you wish for.

Number seven – **A new home?**

Some time had passed and I continued with my occult, as well as other studies. I had become a member of a certain community organization. This was your typical civic effort, at least in appearance. We fought for the rights of others, we fought against injustice, and we endeavor to educate others about the aforementioned. Often times we would have visitors. These visitors were members of the various branches of this same community organization. One day we were meeting with a few visitors from a different branch and these visitors began to tell us about an organization they had joined. This organization was similar to the organization that I was a member of early on; the organization that had proved to be hollow.

Certainly as you can imagine this dialogue is met with reluctance, especially on my part considering my last experience; but after some deliberation I and my colleagues decided to give this new organization a chance.

We attended our first meeting with this new organization; this potential new home. A number of my colleagues were initiated that day. I didn't have to be initiated, because I had already been initiated the past. There was an elderly gentleman who was the head of this organization. There was a bunch of us sitting in a large banquet area waiting to get a glimpse of this elderly statesman. After about 30 minutes of waiting the doors opened and in walks this elderly leader, cloaked in a purple robe. He walked very slow, smiling and waving as he passed each person on his way towards the front of the room. As he reached the front of the room he was greeted by several other slightly older gentlemen who seemed to look upon him with reverence. After shaking hands with the slightly elderly gentlemen, he then turned towards the rest of us in the audience and spoke. He said "peace, my brothers". His voice is very soft and welcoming. His was message delivered very slow and deliberate. I remember thinking, "this is going to be interesting". Even some of my colleagues from my community organization began to look at this leader with reverence as well; it was hard not to. He appeared so regal and knowledgeable. I was feeling a little special because at one point he singled me out giving me praise for my past accomplishments in that similar organization I had mentioned before.

Then, all of a sudden, this sweet, gentle old man transformed! What was once a voice so soft had become thunderous. This elderly leader was yelling and cursing! You would think that such a transformation would cause the listeners to move away; but it was just the opposite. It seemed that this unpredictable change, this display of power further validated his position in the minds of all who were in attendance. I thought "what a spectacle". It was exciting. I thought that I had found a new home.

Unlike the previous hollow organization, of which I was a member; this new organization, this new home of mines actually possessed very valuable and enlightening information. I was very satisfied, or so I thought.

Several months later a couple of colleague of mines and I attended another meeting where this charismatic leader would be speaking. There were only a select number of people who were allowed to attend; this was because the meeting was only for persons who had surpassed a certain level. I and one of my colleagues were passing through the hallway when we encountered a gentleman from the leader's cabinet. This gentleman introduced himself as the chief astrologer for the organization's head man. I and my colleague thought to ourselves "wow". Just imagine how much information about astrology this guy must have if he is the chief astrologer for the entire organization. Naturally we began to ask this chief astrologer questions with the hope that he might provide us a powerful learning experience. But to our dismay we determined immediately that this so-called chief astrologer was no chief at all. This guy began to "educate us" on astrological matters so elementary that we were shocked. In fact his elementary understanding was totally incorrect. My colleague and I could not wait to return to our chapter of this organization and alert them to the fact that the organization's chief astrologer was a dunce.

Two months later I had to travel out of town with a gentleman who was the head of one of the chapters within the organization. When I met up with this gentleman he told me that we were traveling to pick up the organization's leader. I was very excited. Prior to picking up the leader I told the brother that I was traveling with about my encounter with the chief astrologer. Once we picked up the leader the gentlemen begin to tell the leader about my encounter with his chief astrologer. The leader then began to question me on certain astrological principles and he quickly realized that I not only was more learned on the subject than his chief astrologer, but that I was even more learned on the subject than he (the organization's leader) was. The leader then laughed and ordered me to stay away from his chief astrologer. This he did before petitioning me to relocate to the town where he lived in order to become his new chief astrologer. I found that I was simultaneously honored at the request and reluctant regarding relocation. I simply smiled and never responded. The subject was never brought up again. I then realized that I and the gentleman from the other chapter had the responsibility of driving leader back home. This too I thought was an honor. We reached his place and were greeted by his wife. I wasn't too fond of her. Something about her just wasn't authentic. Nonetheless we spent a decent amount of time chatting about the organization and its purpose. The leader began to reveal to us what he qualified as trade secrets, some of which I had become familiar in my own occult studies.

I returned home and was excited to share the information I received with my colleagues. But on returning I learned that my colleagues were growing indifferent to the leader and to the organization, due to the leader's failure to provide our chapter materials for which we had already paid for. After a little back-and-forth we had finally received the materials that we were due, but by this time my colleagues and I had grown totally indifferent and thus had made the decision to depart from this organization and to venture out on our own.

Number eight – **A new direction**

Now that our immediate chapter of this organization was chartered, we set out on our own in search of greater understanding. Over the next few years our membership would double and we would even go on to establish additional chapters of this organization in other cities and in other states. Our organization was essentially the "head" of this new organizational structure.

In retrospect, I realize now that though we were on a quest for clarity, we were actually pretty confused; not only in regards to direction, but also due to an uncertainty about what was in fact true. I myself even begin to question whether there was any information or secrets of real value that this ancient organization was in possession of. One day we were sitting and talking and we made the determination that our new direction or rather our new intent was to identify or find details about the original or very first organization.

We had made the determination that the only way that we could ever truly validate any of the information that we have acquired thus far, was to reach back into history with the hopes of finding and connecting to this organization's source. This marked a very interesting time in my life. Minor confusion about direction; questions about the validity of my associations; questions about purpose or my place in the scheme of things; these types of thoughts began to occupy my mind more often than not. Interestingly enough, I was not discouraged by these thoughts, but was instead further motivated and even more determined to know.

Before discussing what happened next, there is a need for me to provide you certain details that I intentionally omitted early on. I mentioned that I engaged in elemental spiritual practices in an effort to gain a greater understanding. What I did not mention was that my reach out into the void bore fruit. Initially it didn't register. Maybe because I wasn't sensitive enough or insightful enough to notice; but I happened to be at a colleague's apartment one day and we begin to discuss certain elemental spiritual practices. We couldn't have been talking more than 5 minutes before my colleague began giving me books. He handed me 10 books and said "you should read these; in fact, you can have them". I thought this was very generous of him. I took the books home with me, and one by one, I read them all.

This colleague of mines was initially a mere associate of sorts; but after a while I began to notice that the nature of our connection, our interaction had changed. It took a while for me to notice, but I realize that every time I engaged in an elemental spiritual practice in search of greater understanding, this gentleman would somehow be the conduit or the doorway even to the "answers" that I would receive. He was just as clueless as I was about this phenomenon. Using techniques that I learned via my occult practices, I begin to try to find a link between myself and my colleague. After a short time I determined that what I assumed was true; that this gentleman, who was gradually becoming a close friend of mines was in fact, in my opinion, an Oracle sorts for me; for often when I sought answers to questions or when I endeavored to determine a direction, a clue or clues would, in a strange and almost unnoticeable way, come through him. When I finally recognized this pattern I brought it to his attention. Initially his skepticism was noticeable, but even he couldn't deny the irony. Nevertheless, I had made my determination and though still slightly skeptical and rightfully so, he agreed.

Number nine - **Seek, and ye shall watch out!**

I often find myself reflecting on my travels and laughing at the arrogance characterized by man's tendency to become comfortable with what he believes is his progress. At each step in my learning where I encountered a new discovery, my foreword or rather my upward momentum would freeze; similar to energy in matter. My activity would flat-line, due to my mind's preoccupation with what I assumed was THE answer; but soon these assumptions would happen no more. As I warned earlier, be careful what you wish for.

The Storm

One night I was asleep at a girlfriend's house when I was awakened by the sounds of the powerful storm outside. I thought it was strange, because I had never heard the wind sound so strong. I get up out of the bed and I go to the window and what I saw simultaneously amazed and frightened me. I observed heavy rain moving or blowing horizontally! I also observed what I qualified as a greenish-bluish glow amidst the rain. My initial thought of course was that this was some interesting lightening effect. Soon the storm would settle and I returned back to bed. The next morning got up, I got dressed, I headed outside and was floored by what I saw. The entire city was an absolute mess. Trees were everywhere; destroyed by the strong winds of the storm; so much so, that the government declared a state of emergency in the city. After about a week though, our city was clean and back to normal. My reason for mentioning this storm will become clear a little later.

Episode # 1

A few months later I am once again sleep at my girlfriend's house when I am awakened by the strangest experience I've ever had. While sleeping, I begin to hear what I labeled as a screeching sound. I open my eyes to find my feet elevated off of the bed and held by what I can only qualify as some sort of vortex that appeared to be about two to 2 1/2 feet in diameter. Naturally this site startled me. I attempted to sit up, but quickly realized that I could not move. This of course startled me even more. I looked to my right and attempted to raise my hand to nudge my girlfriend, only to be terrified by the fact that I couldn't even move my hand to nudge her. I am in no way ashamed to admit that I was terrified, but believe it or not, I did not panic. Somehow my mind immediately referred back to an elemental practice that I created. And in that moment I applied this practice to my strange circumstance and in no time at all the experience ended. Once I realized that it was over and that I could move I looked over to awaken my girlfriend only to realize that she wasn't even there! She was actually out of town visiting family. I turned to check the time and saw that the clock read 4:20 AM.

The fact that this strange episode took place, coupled with my illusion that my girlfriend was lying next to me caused me to write this episode off as a bad dream.

I remember sharing the story of this experience with my fellow members of my organization. As you can imagine, they too laughed it off as a bad dream.

Episode # 2

One year later, I was asleep in a room on the top floor of the place where I lived and all of a sudden I was awakened by the same screeching sound. This episode was of shorter duration and when I opened my eyes there was no vortex and I was able to move. It was my next observation that surprised me. When I looked at the clock to check the time, it read 4:20 AM! This was strange indeed. What are the chances that at each time I encountered the same experience, the time day or the time of night in this case would be exactly the same?

By the time of this second encounter, as mentioned, it is a year after the first experience and I had a new girlfriend. I recall discussing my experiences with her and her cousin who claimed to be a shaman. This cousin was convinced that the "spirits" were reprogramming me (Ha!). Now, he didn't come up with this idea on his own. Before receiving this "shaman's" diagnosis, I had mentioned to him that almost immediately following each of these two episodes, I would make some kind of mind altering, life changing discovery. It was almost as if my level of awareness had increased tremendously. This was a mere theory of course, but my understanding of certain things had improved so much that it was absolutely impossible to ignore. As I'm sure you can imagine, my thinking changed and so my life, my focus and my direction had once again changed.

Episode #3

This next episode was arguably one of the scariest moments of my life.

I was once again asleep in the room on the top floor in the place where I lived. Amazingly, I could hear the screeching sound faintly in the distance, but increasing in volume and intensity with every passing millisecond. It was as if I was somehow alert, though I was asleep. I mean, how else could I be cognizant that this sound is approaching? I remember thinking (apparently while sleeping) oh no, not again. This episode though, made the other two episodes seem like nothing.

This time the screeching sound became so loud that it was almost deafening. The intensity was so strong that it seemed as if there was something softly brushing against my face. Ha! Imagine my mindset at this moment. I, at the same time, notice what I identified as a flickering or flashing electric-blue light that I could see, though my eyes were still closed. The screeching sound grew so intense that it seemed as if it or something was vibrating and it was this vibrating sensation that I felt against my face. I remember being so afraid that in my dream I yelled, "oh shit!" I was so afraid and I remember thinking "I am not going to open my eyes", because I was afraid of what I might have seen. It was at this moment that I realized that I was actually awake and alert. After an extended moment of what I will qualify as very serious mental torture, the episode ended; not on its own, but because of my using the same elemental practice that I used during my very first episode.

I slowly opened my eyes; looking cautiously to the right and then to my left. Fortunately, I was alone. Considering my last two episodes, I immediately reached for the clock. Yes, you guessed it; 4:20 AM! Okay, I know that I not crazy now. At that moment I realized that, while I thought I might've only yelled in my dream, I apparently yelled out loud, because my yelling had awakened a family member who was in the room just below mines.

This last episode had frightened so much that I did not return to my room for the next few days. I went to stay with another family member. I remember standing in his kitchen and telling him about my episodes. His response to me was, "all right, don't you call that stuff over here". We laughed.

As you can imagine, this last episode caused me to do lots thinking. I noticed that these episodes only took place when I was alone. I also noticed that these episodes only took place when I was lying on my back. I began to do research to see if anyone had reported similar experiences. I found a lot of interesting information, but none of which provided the answers.

I remember a conversation with my Oracle friend where he suggested that something might have been materializing in my room; and that he, at least due to the nature of my descriptions of the event, didn't think that whatever may have been materializing in my room wasn't at all friendly. I agreed. At this point I really begin to question myself. Is there something of a strange nature happening to me? Is there something of a sinister nature trying to get me? Or, is my fear and ignorance causing me to miss out on yet another mind altering, life changing experience? I also wondered if these episodes were in any way related to the strange storm that I mentioned earlier? The very first episode happened only three months after this very strange storm. I never proved this true, but I still wonder about that even today.

Anyway back to my story. I begin to think to myself that I needed to find the courage to confront whatever this thing is, should another episode take place.

Episode # 4

After determining my need for courage I decided to return to my room in hopes of gaining a greater understanding. Once again I am asleep and once again I can hear the screeching sound creeping in the distance. As the sound increases in volume I SNATCHED myself out of sleep. I sit up very quickly and immediately the screeching sounds stopped; Nothing. I giggled to myself and said, "Well, that didn't work". I checked the time and the clock read 4:20 AM.

Quite a bit of time has passed now since my last episode. The unusually unexplainable increases in awareness continued to happen. I couldn't really qualify why I was rapidly becoming "extremely" aware. Reading books had an entirely different meaning now. My ability for interpretation, association, etc. was astounding. After a while I hadn't given the episodes much more thought.

Episode # 5

A few years have passed and I am living in a new place and I am involved in a new relationship. I am once again alone at my new girlfriend's house and I am asleep on her couch in her living room. All of a sudden to my surprise I can hear the infamous screeching sound creeping up in the distance. I immediately opened my eyes. I was lying with a sheer sheet over my face and I can see the mantle through the sheet. I assumed based on my last episode that the sound would stop once I had awakened. I was wrong. I was most certainly wide awake with my eyes wide open and the screeching sound not only continued, but increased in volume. I could hear the sound, but there was nothing there (or at least nothing physical that I could see or touch). The sound became so loud that I reached up and covered my ears. Strangely enough, covering my ears made the sound even louder. Then, just like that, it stopped; this time on its own. I remember not being afraid; I turned and I looked at the clock and as I'm sure you can guess it read 4:20 AM. I then went back to sleep.

Number ten – **Confirmation**

We are now a year or more into the future. My episodes had stopped, never happening again to date. I am sitting in the living room at my own residence wondering about a number of things that I and my Oracle buddy had discussed over the last year or more. Certain findings caused us to wonder about the origin of our people. Our research coupled with my episodes caused us to consider the possibility of a different, more shocking origin.

After a few hours of thinking I decided to return back to my elemental practices, which have up until this point provided me respectable results (comedy). I began preparing a very elaborate practice; so elaborate that I called my Oracle buddy and another to let them know about what I was preparing to do. I reached out to my Oracle buddy and this other person, so that in the event that I appeared unstable in the following days, or worse, that I somehow disappear, they would know what happened; or at least know how it happened. I was not taking any chances considering the experiences I had. What I told them was that I was seeking answers about the origin of "people like us". This practice was to commence the following afternoon.

The next morning as the noon hour approached I received a phone call from my Oracle buddy. He asked me to repeat for him what I said I was endeavoring to do. I repeated as much for him and he began to laugh, because once again my Oracle buddy was the conduit or the connecting agent to the 'where-ever'. My Oracle buddy proceeds to tell me about a book that he just received in the mail. The book came from a gentleman who was involved in an organization similar to the previous two organizations that I was part of. For our purposes let's refer to this gentleman as Mr. X. Mr. X is the author of the book that was sent to my Oracle buddy. This book somehow appears to, not necessarily answer the question that I was 'planning' to ask, but instead provided a method for determining an answer. At this point I was absolutely convinced of two things: one - my Oracle buddy was indeed my 'Oracle' buddy; two - my ability through my elemental practices had become so adept that just my preparation for and thoughts about my intended practice and question was so powerful that it evoked a response before the actual practice had even taken place. Yes, I had my answer.

Not only did I get the answer to my initial question, but I also learned methods of determining a number of things, including the meaning of the screeching sound, my locations during the episodes, the electric blue light, and even 4:20 AM. For example: in a certain alpha-numeric system, 420 becomes 42 when the zero is dropped. 42 is the value of the acronym UFO! The reverse of 42 is of course 24, the value of the word GOD! Maybe God drives a UFO. (jokes) The letters "AM" produces the value '22'. In a certain other alpha numeric system, 20 is the value of a word that means "*to grasp*". 2 is the value of a word that means "*house*". The 22nd and final letter in that code is a word which means "mark". This suggests a High Priest or Bishop; a target and a conduit between 'God' and Earth. Or maybe I am wrong (smile).

I realize that all that I had done; the studying, the research, the elemental practices, had made me a magnate for close encounters of the third kind (and almost of the fourth kind – whew!). I and my Oracle buddy came to the conclusion that the shaman may have been correct, with one difference: that it wasn't necessarily a reprogramming, but maybe more accurately, the downloading and/or maybe the activation of a technology; a technology called Xurek Akun. I can't say that we have validated this assumption, but with all that we have experienced it's most certainly not unfathomable.

I can only speculate about why I specifically needed to know about this thing that others would deny. Maybe the reason was for me to make mention or at least suggest the possibilities of such a thing in this book. Whatever the reason, I wouldn't change my overall experiences nor my insane episodes for anything in the world.

By now you know what I'm about to say; that my thinking and therefore my life would once again forever change and never be the same. I have discovered things and I have done things that most people were conditioned to believe was impossible. Unfortunately, it is not my responsibility to convince you otherwise.

These days my life is much different. The things that are of value to most people have absolutely little to no value for me. My thinking and my method of being has become so foreign to the average person that it is often times of no use even engage.

I never thought that I would share this story with anyone, let alone publish it in a book. My intent was to share my experiences under the consideration that someone else on earth may have had similar experiences; or may currently be living these types of experiences. If by chance this is you, I hope that my story provides you some perspective. As for me, I have learned that life is forever moving and the lessons associated with life are numerous. Complacency is not an option. There is no plateau; onward and upward.

Oh, and one more thing; if I were you, I would keep my eyes peeled for the blue sun.

About the Author

Xurek Akun is fairly new writer of fiction, who has demonstrated an amazing ability to captivate his readers. His work, filled with excitement and adventure is sure to keep his readers returning for more.

Stay tuned for more to come from this talented new author.